Spitfire Mk II A
Red Arrow
NYP
Airbus A380
Eurocopter Twin Squirrel
Concorde
rumman F4F Wildcat
pter Twin Squirrel
Messerschmitt BF 109
Sopwith Camel

For my agent, Laura, with appreciation and warmest thanks.

First published in Great Britain and the USA in 2009 by Frances Lincoln Children's Books,
4 Torriano Mews, Torriano Avenue, London NW5 2RZ
www.franceslincoln.com

British Library Cataloguing in Publication Data available on request

ISBN: 978-1-84507-925-3

Illustrated with pencil, charcoal and watercolour

Printed in China

1 3 5 7 9 8 6 4 2

Louis' Dream Plane

TERRY MILNE

F
FRANCES LINCOLN
CHILDREN'S BOOKS

LOUIS LOVED AEROPLANES.
He loved them more than chocolate, pizza or even watching telly.

Most of all he loved visiting airports and air shows with his grandpa.

He dreamed of becoming a pilot and flying up above the clouds where the sun always shines.

One day at school something caught Louis' eye, something that made his heart leap.

It was a toy Gypsy Moth! And there was no one with it.

Louis spun the propeller and pushed it slowly across the playground, imagining it taxiing towards a runway.

The little wheels rolled faster and faster until. . .

The Gypsy Moth took off
with Louis in the pilot's seat.

The sound of the school bell brought him back to earth with a BUMP!

He ran into the classroom with the Gypsy Moth
tucked under his sweater, his heart pounding
with excitement.

Miss Cartridge's voice droned on, and Louis drifted back into the cockpit of the Gypsy Moth.

"What's that on your desk, Louis?" Miss Cartridge's voice cut into his dream, sharp as a seagull's cry.

"It's . . . my toy Gypsy Moth," stammered Louis.

Charlie leapt up, exclaiming, "It's mine, Miss Cartridge." But just at that moment an ambulance raced past with sirens wailing, distracting Miss Cartridge. She put the little plane in her drawer and carried on with the lesson. Louis flushed, but said nothing.

"I don't want to see this in class again," Miss Cartridge said, as she gave Louis the Gypsy Moth at the end of school.

It was the last day of term so he ran home,
as fast as a Red Arrow.

He was glad he didn't see Charlie.

All afternoon Louis flew the Gypsy Moth
round the world of his room.

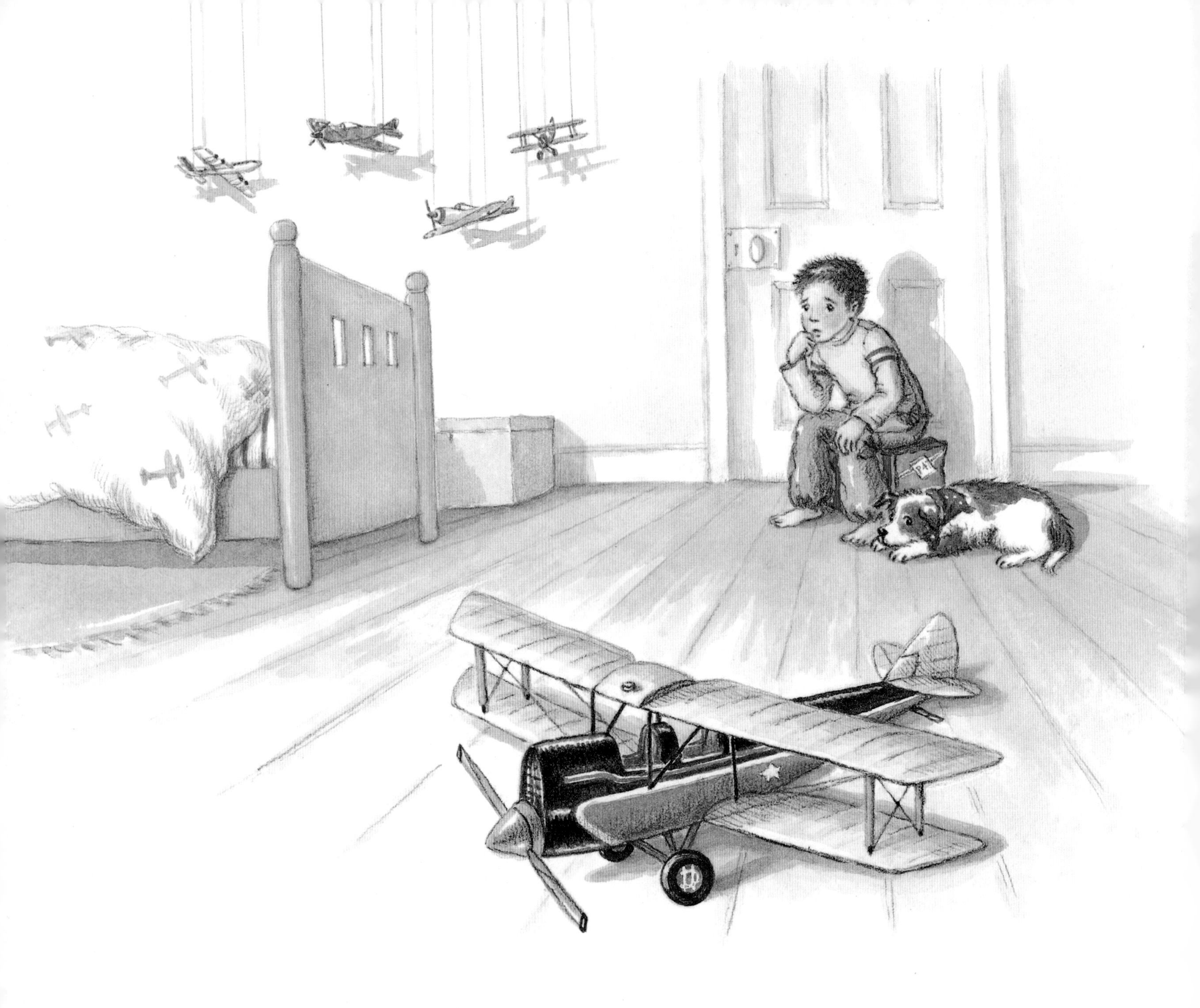

But as the days passed, Louis had less fun playing with the Gypsy Moth, knowing all the time that it belonged to Charlie.

Still, he couldn't bear to lose it, so one day he made a hangar on top of his cupboard and hid it there.

On the first day of term, Louis took the little plane out of its hiding place. He was determined to give it back to Charlie.

Louis got to school early. He ran inside to find Charlie . . . but Charlie wasn't there.

The bell rang, and still Charlie didn't come.

Then Miss Cartridge told the class that Charlie's family had moved, and that Charlie wouldn't be coming to their school any more.

Louis' heart sank.

When he walked home that afternoon he felt as deflated as a windsock on a windless day.

By the time he got home, Louis could bear it no longer.

"Do you still have Charlie's mum's email address from the time you ran the cake stall together?" he burst out when he saw his mother.

"I do!" said his mum. "Why? What's the matter?"

Louis told his mum all about the Gypsy Moth.

Luckily, Charlie's mum responded to their email straightaway.

That very Saturday they set off to see Charlie, who had not moved far away.

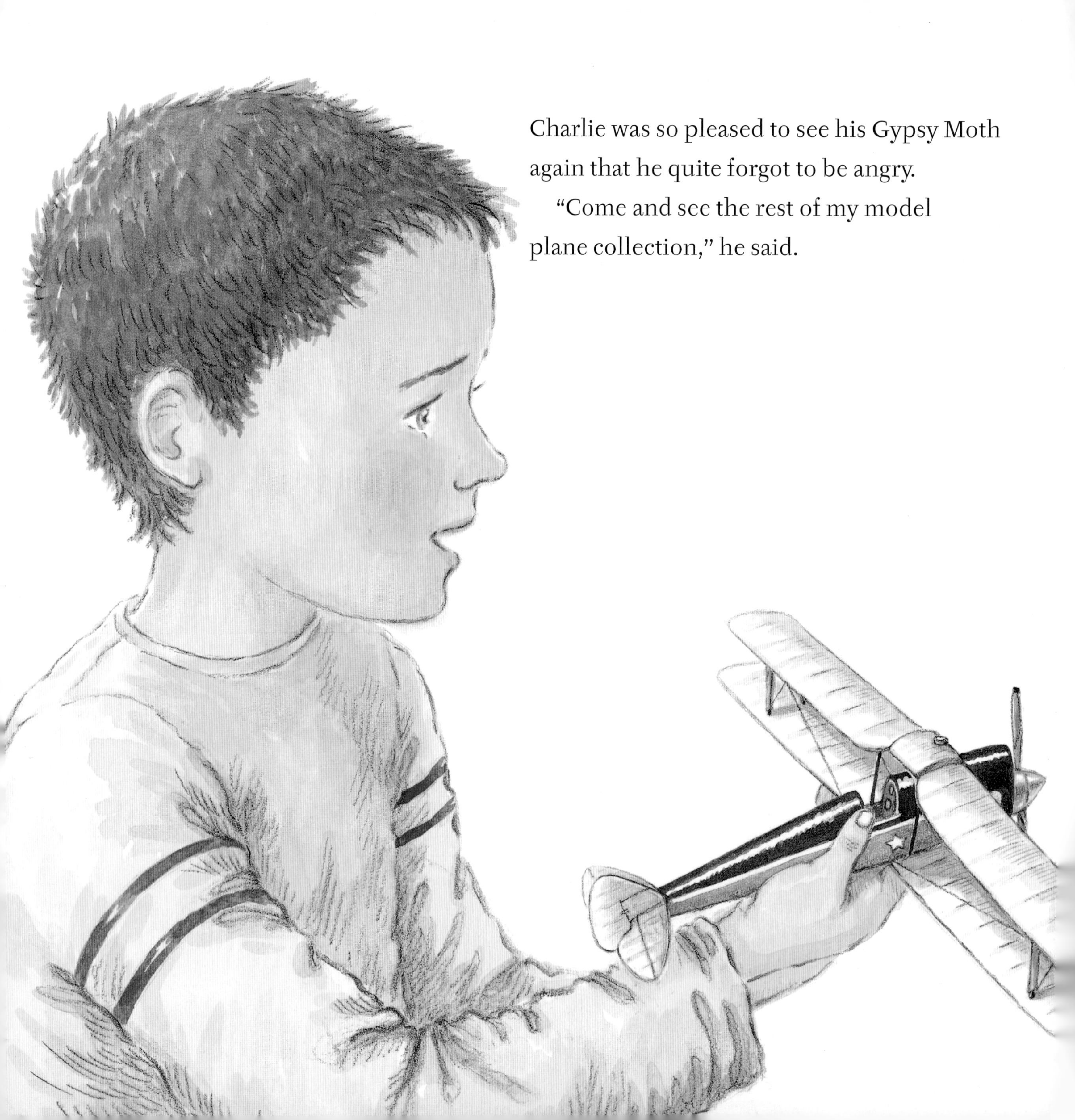

Charlie was so pleased to see his Gypsy Moth again that he quite forgot to be angry.

"Come and see the rest of my model plane collection," he said.

Louis felt a great weight
lift off his shoulders
and he glided into the
house behind Charlie.

"LOOK!"

cried Charlie.

They spent the rest
of the day playing
with Charlie's aeroplanes
and sharing the
magic of flying.

Charlie gave Louis a model Gypsy Moth kit for his birthday and they built it together.

The Gypsy Moth is now Louis' favourite plane.

It's the reason he and Charlie became friends . . .

and that's better than
all the model aeroplanes in the world.

Spitfire MK II A
Sopwith Camel
Bleriot XI Monoplane
Thunderbolt P47
Fokker DR-I Triplane
Red Arrow
The Wright Brothers'
Fokker DR-I Triplane
Spitfire MK II A
Messerschmitt BF 109
Boeing 747